Love Letters

Dedicated to the internet, for showing me these things.
And to Char, for at least discussing letting me try them.

First published in the United Kingdom in 2008 by
Portico Books
10 Southcombe Street
London
W14 0RA

An imprint of Anova Books Company Ltd

Copyright © Jack Noel, 2008

The moral right of the author has been asserted.

ISBN 978-1-906032-60-9

A CIP catalogue record for this book is available from the British Library.

10 9 8 7 6 5 4 3 2 1

Printed and bound by Imago, Thailand.

This book can be ordered direct from the publisher. Contact the marketing department, but try your bookshop first.

www.anovabooks.com

www.jacknoel.co.uk

Love Letters

Jack Noel

PORTICO

Foreword from the Author's Mother

It is with great maternal pride I write to introduce this first work by my first born, *Love Letters*. Or at least, it kind of is. Having your son publish a book like this is like being given a winning scratchcard covered in shit: you do want it, of course you do. But it's still disgusting.

I am proud my son has a book. After all, I can say "My Jack? Why, he's a published author." Indeed I often do. It certainly gives my opinions an extra gravitas at the Queens Park Book Group. I'm just not proud that it's a filthy, disgusting, rabbit-sex book. It was pretty awkward explaining the ins and outs of the *Rusty Trombone* to the group, let me tell you. (Though Jill was surprisingly *au fait* with *Pearl Necklaces*... perhaps she has something to get off her chest.)

As a parent, one feels compelled to attribute all of their child's character traits back to some influential experience in their formative years. The rudimentary linework in this book, for example, makes it clear that my son grew up studying the wrong Leonardo, Raphael, Michaelangelo and Donatello. But what gross parenting error made him so… well, gross? We tried to do everything right. We served him Alphabetti Spaghetti to broaden his burgeoning vocabulary. If I'd only known it would end up being this broad I would have at least taken out some of the Xs. Perhaps we shouldn't have let him see us making tea in the mug. Or playing the bagpipes. Or eating cream pie. Or perhaps there is nothing we could have done. Nature or nurture, so much sex just isn't natural.

So thank you for looking at my son's book. Isn't it just lovely? But please, read it no further. Isn't it just awful?

Yours proudly/ashamedly,

Jack's Mum

Letters

A is for Alcohol

is for

Bagpiping

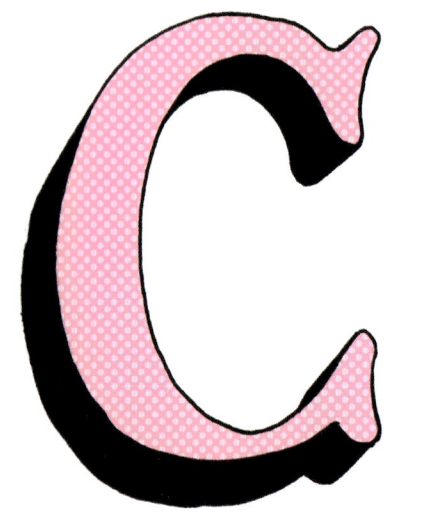

is for

Creampie

is for

Dogging

E is for Emetophilia

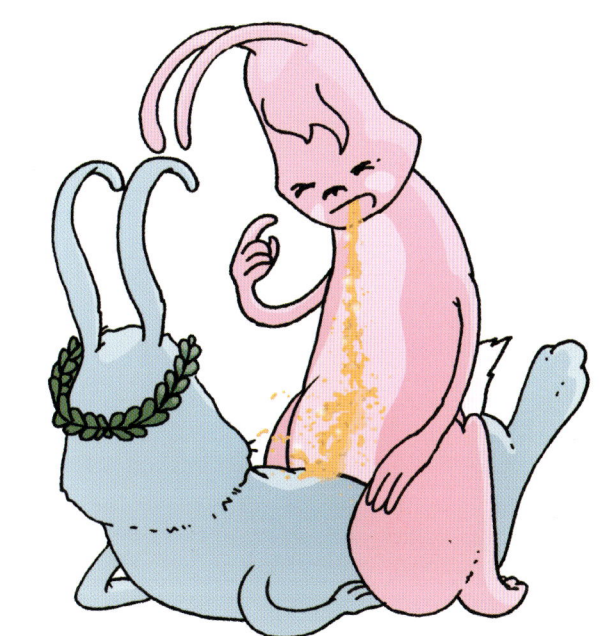

is for

Felching

is for

Golden

Shower

is for

Hentai

is for

Interspeciality

is for

Jerking
Off

is for
Klismaphilia

is for

Lap dancing

is for

Masochism

is for

Nasolingus

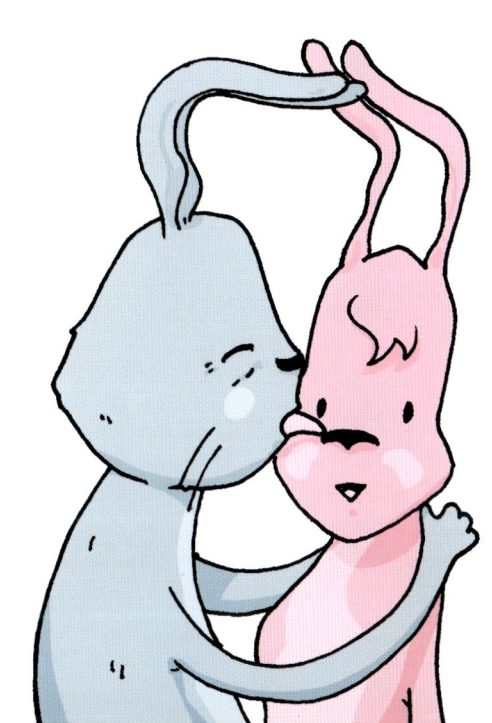

is for

Pearl

Necklace

is for

Queefing

is for

Snowballing

is for
Teabagging

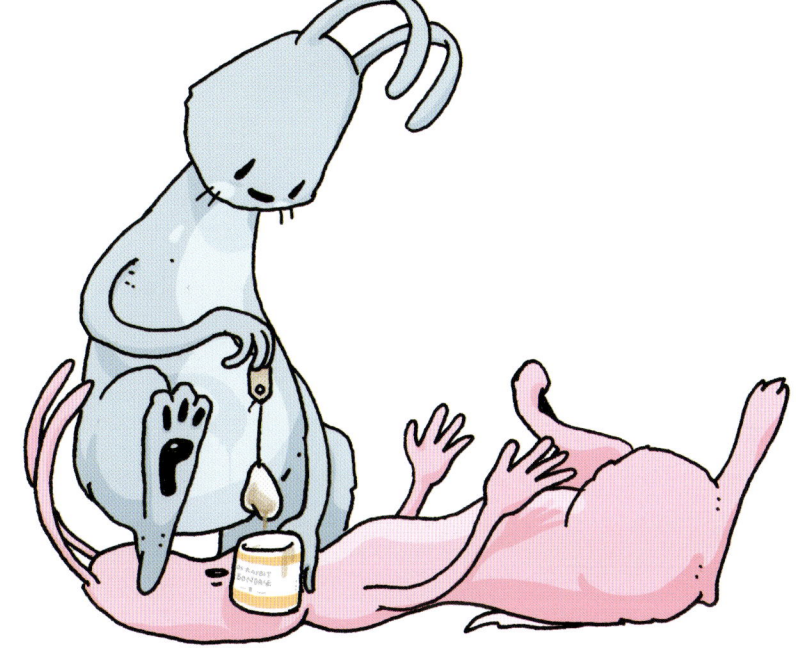

is for

Underwear

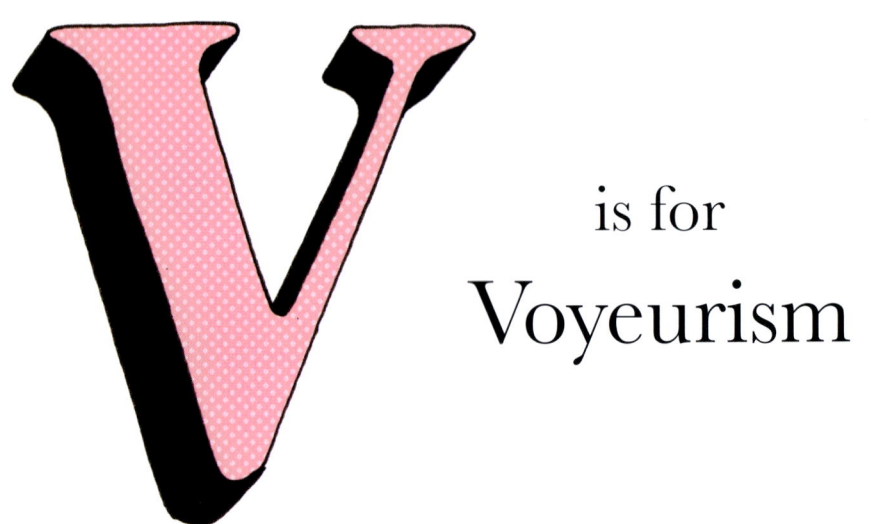

is for

Voyeurism

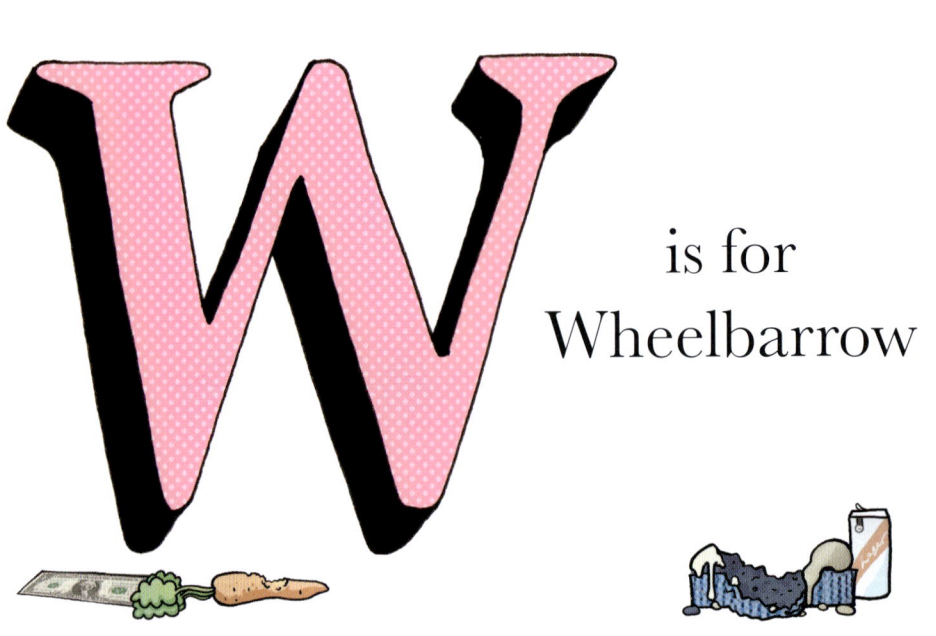

W is for Wheelbarrow

is for

X-rated

is for

Yoke

is for…

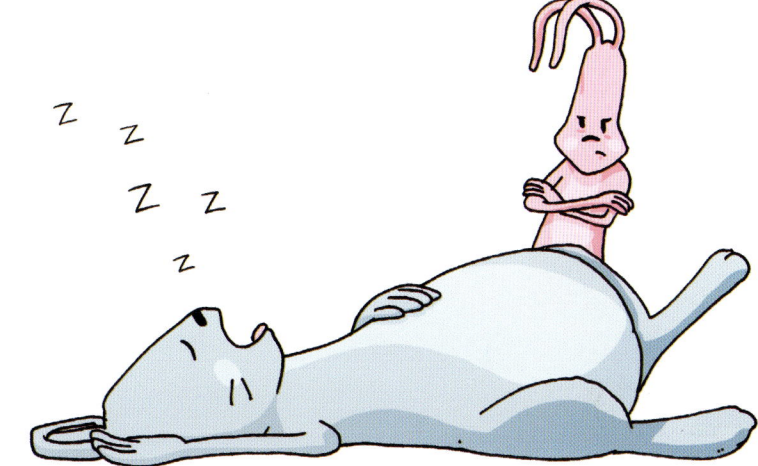

Glossary

Al•co•hol *n.* Legal drug that makes trying things easier but doing them more difficult. Popular almost universally esp. with the unemployed, the taxman and the French.

Bag•pip•ing 1. *v.* Playing the bagpipes 2. *v.* Axilliary intercourse; sex with the armpit. A tiny bit like *1.* ie. generally found to be unpleasant.

Cream•pie 1. *n.* A pie of cream 2. *v.* The act of ejaculating inside ones partner 3. *n.* The result of *2.*, which looks a tiny bit like *1.* though tastes a lot saltier.

Dogg•ing *v.* Engaging in or spectating upon sexual acts in semi-public places. Named for practitioners – ostensibly walking pets in the vicinity – generally being of low attractiveness.

Em•et•o•phil•ia *n.* Deriving sexual pleasure from Roman Showers ie. vomiting on/being vomited on by people—which are neither as civilised nor as hygienic as their name suggests.

Felch•ing *v.* An onomatopoeia for sucking semen, preferably one's own, out of an orifice. Eating a *Creampie*.

Gold•en Show•er *n.* Watersports. Neither as glamorous nor as hygienic as the name suggests.

Hentai *n.* Sexually explicit cartoons.

Jerk•ing Off *n.* Handy stimulation.

Klis•ma•phil•ia *n.* Deriving sexual pleasure from the introduction of liquids to the rectum. Popular with those who keep their friends close and enemas closer.

Lap•danc•ing *v.* Sexy dancing on and around the recipient, who laps it up.

Mas•o•chis•m *n.* Deriving sexual gratification being treated like an egg ie. whipped, cracked and beaten.

Nas•o•ling•us *n.* Nose licking. Not to be confused with *nasalingus* (astronaut licking).

Org•y *n.* Sex involving more than two participants simultaneously.

Popular in Ancient Rome and the home counties. Actually quite depressing.

Pearl Neck•lace 1. *v.*   A necklace of pearls. 2. *n.*   The result of a man ejaculating on a neck. Looks a tiny bit like *1.*, but is less keenly received.

Queef•ing *v.*   Onomatopoeic term for vaginal flatulence. Sounds a tiny bit like a normal fart but smells different.

Rust•y Trom•bone 1. *n.*   An aged brass instument. 2. *n.*   Sexual act in which anilingus and masturbation are performed simultaneously. Feels (and tastes) a tiny bit like playing *1.*

Snow•ball•ing *n.* The act of swapping semen in the mouth via a French kiss. Ironically very warm and loving.

Tea•bagg•ing *v.*   The act of dipping scrotum in someone's face – a tiny bit like one might a teabag in a mug.

Und•er•wear *n.*   Lingerie; bras and pants. (But not socks.)

Voy•eur•ism *n.*   Deriving sexual pleasure from observing others.

Wheel•barrow *n.* Sexual position in which one partner is walked around on their hands, possibly carrying a load on their back.

X-rat•ed *n.* Obscene materials for the lonely. Popular with all internet users.

Yoke *n.* Bondage kit that holds the hands up and away from the head. Popular with Oxen.

Z•z•z•z *n.* Widely recognised onomatopoeic device representing snoring. Popular with adult aebecedarians.

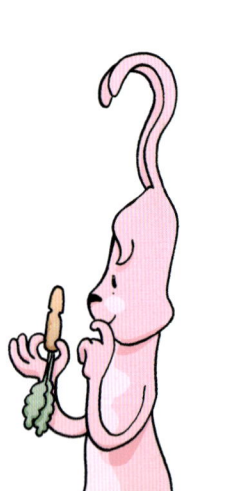

Z
Z
Z
Z